McBROOM
and the
Beanstalk

by Sid Fleischman

Illustrated by Walter Lorraine

An Atlantic Monthly Press Book
Little, Brown and Company
BOSTON   TORONTO

Books by Sid Fleischman

Mr. Mysterious and Company	*The Wooden Cat Man*
By the Great Horn Spoon!	*The Ghost on Saturday Night*
The Ghost in the Noonday Sun	*Mr. Mysterious's Secrets of Magic*
Chancy and the Grand Rascal	*McBroom Tells a Lie*
Longbeard the Wizard	*Me and the Man on the Moon-Eyed Horse*
Jingo Django	*McBroom and the Beanstalk*

TEXT COPYRIGHT © 1978 BY ALBERT S. FLEISCHMAN

ILLUSTRATIONS COPYRIGHT © 1978 BY WALTER H. LORRAINE

FIRST EDITION

T 04/78

Library of Congress Cataloging in Publication Data

Fleischman, Albert Sidney.
  McBroom and the beanstalk.

  "An Atlantic Monthly Press book."
  SUMMARY: McBroom gets ready to tell his many pre-
posterous stories in the World Champion Liar's contest
only to be disqualified for telling the truth.
  [1. Humorous stories] I. Lorraine, Walter H.
II. Title.
PZ7.F5992Maam   [Fic]   77-22177
ISBN 0-316-28570-6

ATLANTIC-LITTLE, BROWN BOOKS
ARE PUBLISHED BY
LITTLE, BROWN AND COMPANY
IN ASSOCIATION WITH
THE ATLANTIC MONTHLY PRESS

Published simultaneously in Canada
by Little, Brown & Company (Canada) Limited

PRINTED IN THE UNITED STATES OF AMERICA

For Clyde
For Judy

Never and no sir! Me enter the World Champion Liar's Contest at the county fair? Why, hair'll grow on fish before I trifle with the truth.

"But Pa," said our oldest girl, Jill. "You might win a blue ribbon."

The young'uns looked up from their breakfast plates and joined in.

"Sure, Pa!"

"Go ahead!"

"Make up a real whopper!"

I held up my hand to stop the clamor. "Bless my suspender buttons!" I declared. "You'd have your pa known as a blue ribbon, first prize, world champion *liar?* I'm surprised at you. Why, I couldn't hold my head up."

"Of course, Pa," my dear wife Melissa said. "But the contest is all in fun."

"Never, nohow and notwithstanding," I snapped. "And let that be the end of it."

The young'uns had hardly gone out to play when they came flocking back in.

"Will*jill*hester*chester*peter*polly*tim*tom*mary*larry*andlittle*clarinda!*" said my wife. "I'd dearly appreciate it if you could go out and come in without slamming the screen door twenty-two times."

"But Ma! Pa! Come look! Quick!"

Outside they pointed to a wet footprint in our wonderful one-acre farm. Merciful powers! That wasn't any common footprint. A hog could wallow in the big toe alone.

"I'll be thundered," I said. "That's the biggest, big-footed, flat-footed, bony-footed footprint I ever laid eyes on."

"A giant made it," Chester said.

"Fe, fi, fo, fum," said Little Clarinda.

"I'm scared," Polly muttered. "Maybe the giant was looking in our windows last night."

I squinted over the prairie. No other footprints of a giant out for a stroll. I began to chuckle. "Nothing to be scared of, my lambs. Isn't this topsoil of ours so rip-snorting rich anything'll grow in it? And quicker'n lickety-toot. Wasn't there a whistle of rain last evening? I calculate someone planted that footprint and it just grew in the night."

Why, only last month Mary forgot her pile

of jacks, and next morning it had grown into a jungle gym. We hauled it over to the school yard for everyone to play on.

"I wish it *was* a giant," Chester declared.

I did wonder who had been pussyfooting around the farm last night. "We'd best fill in the footprint and rake it over before it grows any bigger," I said. "And then I'm going to town for a haircut. County fair's tomorrow."

The barbershop was full up. And there in the spare barber chair sat Judge Honest Jim Rattlefinger with his hat on and a gavel in his hand.

"Howdy, Josh McBroom," he said. "We're holding tryouts for the liar's contest. You're next."

Judge Honest Jim himself an official of the contest? I declare if that didn't throw a different light on things. But confound it, I didn't know a single falsehood to tell. "I just came for a snip of barbering," I said.

"You can get your hair butchered and whip us up some flamdoodle at the same time," the judge laughed.

I got in the other chair and Willard, the barber, threw a cloth around me. He began snipping away and I began thinking about our prairie weather. Glory be—I had it!

"Judge and gents," I said. "You recall the pestiferous dust storm that came along last week. Well, it was so dreadful *thick* out our way that we had to put the air through the

12

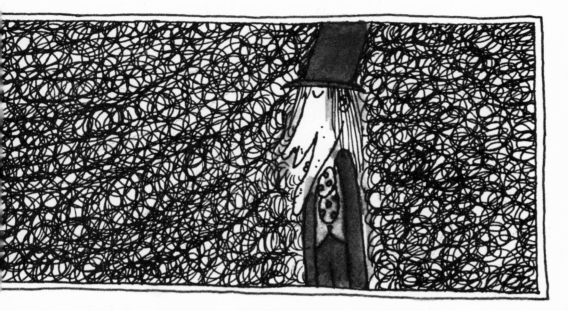

clothes wringer before we could breathe it."

There was a gust of laughter, and I felt almighty proud of myself for rising to the occasion. But I had failed to notice that our infernal neighbor, Heck Jones, had slipped through the crowded doorway.

"Hee-haw, indeed," he snorted. That man was so skinny he couldn't cast a shadow without standing next to someone else. "Don't think you are going to palm off the *truth* in a lyin' contest. That's cheating, McBroom."

13

"Cheating?" I answered, bristling.

"Why, I saw you cranking that dust storm through your clothes wringer. I swear you near cranked me through with it."

Judge Honest Jim Rattlefinger banged his gavel on the arm of the barber chair. "That disqualifies you, McBroom. Who's next, gents?"

I was caught speechless. I glared at Heck Jones. Doggone it, that man was as shy of the truth as a snake is of mittens.

"Hold on, Heck Jones," I said, as a fresh

idea came to mind. "I suppose you saw it the time it rained so hard over our one-acre farm that the water stood fifteen feet and ten inches out of the well." I paused. "It happened in the *pitch-dark of night*."

"Hee-haw," Heck Jones cackled. "If it was so dark in all that pour-down of rain, how did you see it?"

"I lit a match."

"Well, I'm surprised you didn't notice me, McBroom. I was lighting matches too."

Tarnation! That man was slippery as a greased pig. Judge Honest Jim wagged his head and struck the gavel. "Disqualified again, McBroom! You don't seem to have the knack of departing from the honest facts."

Ambling home I felt mad enough to kick a skunk. I did kick up heaps of dirt — and all over two broken-nosed strangers who came slinking around the side of the bank. They began to beat the dust out of their brown derby hats.

"You cuss-fired prairie dog!" one of them growled.

I offered to help shake out their coats, but they slunk away and were gone without another word.

I continued on my way, kicking up dust devils. Heck Jones had got the best of me — blast his scrawny, long-necked, flat-footed hide.

I stopped in a cloud of dust. Flat-footed!

At the supper table I said, "It was Heck Jones left the footprint that grew into that golly-whopper. No one else in the county has bony-footed, flat-footed trotters like his." I wondered what mischief he'd been up to in the night.

"Shuckins," Chester said. He was sorely disappointed. "I'd mighty like to see a genuine giant."

And Little Clarinda said, "Pa, you reckon there's really a fe-fi-fo-fum giant livin' on the clouds?"

I shrugged. "If you young'uns are so set on a giant—well, plant yourself a beanstalk and see if anything climbs down."

"Could we, Pa!" Chester exclaimed. "Wouldn't eyes pop if we could show him at the county fair? He'd take a heap of prizes. The footrace, for certain."

"And the pie-eating contest!" Polly said.

"Well, I won't be going along," I announced.

"I couldn't show my face. Not with folks thinking that Josh McBroom is so dreadful low he'd tried to cheat his way into the World Champion Liar's Contest."

For the first time I told them what had happened in Willard's barbershop. My dear wife Melissa shook her head. "I declare, Pa, just because Heck Jones is so mean that oughten to keep you from going to the fair."

"Never, nohow and notwithstanding," I said.

After morning chores, the young'uns got into their best Sunday clothes. Suddenly the house began to shake and rumble and the dishes rattled.

"What on earth—" I muttered.

"It must be the giant!" Chester said, and rushed to the window.

"What giant?" I exclaimed.

"The fe-fi-fo-fum giant," said Little Clarinda.

"We pitched a bean seed out the window, Pa," Mary said.

We flocked outside. Mercy! The beanstalk

was shooting up quicker'n chain lightning with a link broke. And weren't the roots gorging on our splendiferous topsoil! They had the whole acre to themselves and the ground was heaving and rolling. It near made us seasick to stand there.

Up and upward that vine sprouted—and
then, horrors! The young'uns had forgot to
stake it. The vine flopped over, limp as a
neck-wrung chicken.

But did it stop growing? Not a lick. It took
off down the road like a stepped-on cat, heading straight for town.

"Willjillhesterchesterpeterpollytimtom-
marylarryandlittleclarinda!" I yelled. "Grab
on! Hold it back!"

The stalk was swelling up thick as a tree
trunk.

"Pa!" my dear wife Melissa shouted. "The
roots have got to the well and sucked it dry."

25

"Fetch my ax!"

The young'uns had caught hold of that runaway vine and pulled like a tug-of-war. But there was no holding the thing back. It pulled them off their feet and carried them flying down the road.

I swung the ax. I took a mere chip out of

the stout stalk and axed it again. But, tarnation! The vine was growing so fast I couldn't hit the same spot twice.

I started up our Franklin automobile. My dear wife jumped in and we chased down the road. We caught up to the young'uns and plucked 'em to safety. Peter didn't want to

let go. He was enjoying that prairie sleigh ride.

By then the beanstalk had reached the main street of town. There was not a soul about—everyone was off to the fair. Willard had hung a closed sign in the window, but left his barbershop wide open. My stars! The

28

rambunctious vine charged through the front
door and out the back.

Then it slithered up the stairs of the Corn-
husker's Hotel and came whipping out a
second-story window, carrying two rocking
chairs. It hardly touched ground before it
headed for the blacksmith shop across the

29

street. My, the plunder it was gathering up!

I hoped it would miss the bank—but no. It
rammed through the window with the blacksmith's anvil and out it came, dragging two
customers who must have got locked inside.
I declare if it wasn't the two broken-nosed
fellers in brown derby hats. My, how bad luck

was following them around! I'd kicked dust
over them, they'd got locked in, and now they
had the misfortune to get coiled up in the
greenery.

But worse! That stampeding stalk carried
them off to the jailhouse and left them
tangled up in a cell. I would have stopped to

31

help the unfortunate chaps, but mercy! The vine was heading out of town toward the fairgrounds.

"Hang on, everyone!" I shouted, and off we roared in the car. I took a shortcut along the shallow riverbed and beat that infernal vine by a mile.

We jumped out of the Franklin and shoved through the crowd.

"Trouble a-comin'!" I shouted, but no one paid any attention with so much going on at the fair. Heck Jones was selling dippers of muddy water out of a barrel.

"Genuine hair restorer, gents!" he was calling out. "Step up for Heck Jones's Secret Double-Strength Bald-Headed Elixir! Guaranteed to grow hair on a hen's egg."

I rushed past him to the platform where Judge Honest Jim Rattlefinger was standing with the mayor and the sheriff. They were about to pass out a blue ribbon.

"Run for cover!" I shouted. "A beanstalk's heading straight for the fair!"

"What's that?" said Judge Honest Jim. "A beanstalk?" Everyone broke into a laugh.

I hopped up the platform steps and waved my arms. "Neighbors, trouble's heading this way, and that's the honest truth! The young'uns planted a bean in our wonderful one-acre farm and that seed sprouted like an earthquake. The vine's a giant, I tell you! It took off down the road so all-fired fast it scorched the earth underneath. It went through town like a giant's darning needle, sewing the buildings together. It even locked two strangers in your jail cell, Sheriff. You'll find them tied up in rocking chairs and horse-shoes wrapped around their necks. And I de-clare, the vine must have carried off lather and a razor from Willard's barbershop. The last time I saw those gents their heads were shaved like common criminals. And now that wildcat vine is heading right for us. Grab your women and children and run!"

Mercy! Folks were laughing so hard they wouldn't move. The judge and the mayor and the sheriff were chuckling and muttering among themselves.

Then Judge Honest Jim said, "Josh McBroom, we declare you the blue ribbon winner of the World Champion Liar's Contest. Why, we wouldn't believe your story if we saw that monster vine with our own eyes."

"Then put on your specs, Judge. For here it comes!"

Well, you never saw folks scatter so fast in so many directions. Except for Heck Jones.

"*Hee-haw*," he snorted, not believing me. His back was turned as the vine came whipping along. It caught him up and carried him off. The barrel of hair grower too.

I fetched axes at the wood-chopping contest and stationed the young'uns in a row. We

all took a chop at the stalk, hitting the same
spot as it whizzed by.

Glory be! We hacked the stalk in two.

That didn't exactly stop the cursed thing
in its tracks. But it did take the gumption
out of it. Before long the runaway vine lay
there like a tuckered-out dog. The leaves

began to curl in the sun. It was a good twenty minutes before anyone would go near the thing.

"Gents," I said to the judge and the mayor and the sheriff. "I can't accept this blue ribbon for telling the genuine truth in a liar's contest."

"I expect not," said Judge Honest Jim. "But we're going to pin blue ribbons on your young'uns. No doubt about it. They grew the biggest beanstalk in the history of this county."

A photographer took a picture of the young'uns with as much of the vine as he could get in the picture. Later, they allowed everyone to saw up the stalk for winter firewood. Some folks dragged home the pods, varnished them, and used them for canoes.

Of course, we had to pay for the damage the vine had done in town. But glory be, that was no problem at all. As soon as the sheriff got back to his jail, he found the Broken-Nose Brothers tied up in the cell. I declare if they weren't bank robbers, and a reward offered for them, too!

It was nightfall before Heck Jones turned up. The vine had carried him so far, heels over head, he had a mighty long walk back.

It was no mystery to me now what his foot-print was doing on our farm. He'd stolen half a barrel of our wondrous topsoil to make his elixir.

And my, it did work wonders. The barrel of hair grower had spilled out in the lake behind the fairgrounds. Plenty of fish in the lake. But you couldn't eat one before stopping off at Willard's barbershop to have it shaved.